eOR Rabbit

WOL

Piglet

MEET ALL THESE FRIENDS IN BUZZ BOOKS:

Thomas the Tank Engine
The Animals of Farthing Wood
Biker Mice from Mars
Fireman Sam
Rupert
Babar

First published in Great Britain 1994 by Buzz Books
an imprint of Reed Children's Books
Michelin House, 81 Fulham Road, London SW3 6RB
and Auckland, Melbourne, Singapore and Toronto
Reprinted 1995 (twice)
Copyright © 1994 Michael John Brown, Peter Janson-Smith,
Roger Hugh Vaughan Charles Morgan and
Timothy Michael Robinson, Trustees of the Pooh Properties.
Published under licence from The Walt Disney Company.
Adapted from *Winnie-the-Pooh*, first published 1926 and
The House at Pooh Corner, first published 1928.
Text by A.A. Milne and line drawings by E.H. Shepard
Copyright under the Berne Convention.
Adaptation of the line illustrations and colouring by Arkadia
copyright © 1994 Reed International Books Limited
All rights reserved
ISBN 1 855 91430 1
Printed in Italy

Winnie-the-Pooh
and the honey bees

From the stories by
A.A. Milne

One day, when
he was out walking,
Winnie-the-Pooh came to
a large oak tree. From the top
of the tree there came a loud
buzzing noise.

Winnie-the-Pooh sat down at the foot of the tree; he put his head between his paws and began to think.

First of all he said to himself, "You don't get a buzzing noise like that, just buzzing and buzzing, without it meaning something. The only reason for making a buzzing noise that *I* know of is because you're a bee."

Then he thought another long time and said, "And the only reason for being a bee that I know of is making honey."

And then he got up and said, "And the only reason for making honey is so that *I* can eat it.

"He began
to climb
the tree.
   He
climbed
and he climbed
and he climbed,
and as he climbed
he sang a little
song to himself.
It went like this:

"Isn't it funny
   How a bear
likes honey?
   Buzz! Buzz! Buzz!
   I wonder why
he does?"

He was nearly there now and if he just
stood on that branch... *Crack!*

"Oh, help!" said Pooh, as he spun round
three times and flew gracefully into a
gorse bush, "it all comes of *liking* honey
so much. Oh, help!"

He crawled out of the gorse bush, brushed the prickles from his nose and began to think again. The first person he thought of was Christopher Robin.

So Winnie-the-Pooh went round to his friend Christopher Robin, who lived in another part of the forest.

"Good morning, Christopher Robin," he said. "I wonder if you've got such a thing as a balloon about you?"

"What do you want a balloon for?"
asked Christopher Robin.

Winnie-the-Pooh looked round to see
that nobody was listening and said in a
deep whisper, *"Honey!"*

"But you don't get honey with balloons!"

"I do," said Pooh.

Well, it just happened that Christopher Robin had two balloons; he had a blue one  and a green one.

"Which one would you like?" he asked.

Winnie-the-Pooh put his head between his paws and thought very carefully.

"It's like this," he said. "When you go after honey with a balloon, you mustn't let the bees know you're coming."

"Wouldn't they notice you underneath the balloon?" asked Christopher Robin.

"You never can tell with bees," said Winnie-the-Pooh. "I know. I shall look like a small black cloud floating in the sky. That will deceive them." He chose the blue balloon.

So Christopher Robin and Pooh both went out with the blue balloon, and Winnie-the-Pooh went to a very muddy place that he knew of and rolled and rolled until he was covered with mud.

The balloon was blown up as big as big, and Christopher Robin and Pooh were both holding on to the string. Then Christopher Robin let go suddenly and Pooh Bear floated gracefully up into the sky and stayed there.

"Hooray!" shouted
Christopher Robin.

"Isn't that fine?" called Winnie-the-Pooh. "What do I look like?"

"You look like a bear holding on to a balloon," said Christopher Robin.

"Not," said Pooh
anxiously, " – not like
a small black cloud in a blue sky?"

"Not very much."

"Ah, well, perhaps from up here
it looks different and, as I say,
you never can tell with bees."

There was no wind to blow him nearer
to the tree so there he stayed. He could
see the honey, he could smell the honey
but he couldn't quite reach the honey.

"Christopher Robin!" he said
in a loud whisper.

"Hallo!"

"I think the bees
suspect something!"

"Perhaps they think that
you're after their honey?"

"It may be that. You never
can tell with bees."

There was another little silence, and then he called down again.

"Christopher Robin, have you an umbrella in your house?"

"I think so."

"I wish you would bring it out here, and walk up and down with it, and look up at me every now and then and say 'Tut-tut, it looks like rain.' I think, if you did that, it would help the deception which we are practising on these bees."

Christopher Robin laughed to himself, "Silly old Bear!" but he didn't say it aloud because he was so fond of Pooh.

So he went home for his umbrella.

When Christopher Robin returned,
Winnie-the-Pooh said, "Now, if you walk
up and down with your umbrella, I shall
sing a little Cloud Song, such as
a cloud might sing."
So while Christopher Robin walked up
and down and wondered if it would rain,
Winnie-the-Pooh
sang this song:

"How sweet to be a cloud
Floating in the blue!
Every little cloud
Always sings aloud."

"How sweet to be a cloud
Floating in the blue!
It makes him very proud
To be a little cloud."

The bees were still buzzing
as suspiciously as ever.
Some of them left their nests
and flew all round the cloud
as it began the second verse
of this song, and one bee
sat down on the nose
of the cloud for a moment,
and then got up
again.

"Christopher – *ow!* – Robin," called out
the cloud. "I have come to a very
important decision. *These are the wrong
sort of bees.*"

"Are they?"

"Quite the wrong sort," said Pooh.

"These bees make the wrong sort of honey," declared Winnie-the-Pooh.

"I think I shall come down."

"How?" asked Christopher Robin.

Winnie-the-Pooh hadn't thought about this. If he let go of the string, he would fall – *bump* – and he didn't like the idea of that.

Then he heard a hissing noise coming from the balloon.

The balloon had a hole in it!

Slowly,

Winnie-the-Pooh

floated

down

to

the

ground.

Pooh

Kanga

Christopher Robin